JOIN US NOW!

Carmel Reilly

NELSON
CENGAGE Learning

Australia • Brazil • Japan • Korea • Mexico • Singapore • Spain • United Kingdom • United States

Join Up Now!

Fast Forward
Blue Level 10

Text: Carmel Reilly
Editor: Johanna Rohan
Design: Vonda Pestana
Series design: James Lowe
Production controller: Hanako Smith
Photo research: Corrina Tauschke
Audio recordings: Juliet Hill, Picture Start
Spoken by: Matthew King and Abbe Holmes

Acknowledgements
The author and publisher would like to acknowledge
permission to reproduce material from the following sources:
Photographs by Newsphotos.com/Tom Campbell, p 7/ Ian
Cook, p 4/ Brett Costello, back cover, p 6/ Mark Evans, p 5
top/ Richard Hatherly, cover, pp 1, 13/ Stephen Laffer, p 5
bottom right/ Stuart Mcevoy, p 10/ Steve Morenos, p 14/
Calum Robertson, p 5 bottom left/ Steve Tanner, p 11;
Photolibrary.com/Superstock, Inc, p 9 top; Photolibrary.
com/Age fotostock/Esbin Anderson, p 8/ Fabio Cardoso, p 12/
Dennis MacDonald, pp 8–9/ Ben Welsh, p 15.

ISBN 978 0 17 012547 5
ISBN 978 0 17 012537 6 (set)

Cengage Learning Australia
Level 7, 80 Dorcas Street
South Melbourne, Victoria Australia 3205
Phone: 1300 790 853

Cengage Learning New Zealand
Unit 4B Rosedale Office Park
331 Rosedale Road, Albany, North Shore NZ 0632
Phone: 0508 635 766

For learning solutions, visit cengage.com.au

Printed in Australia by Liagre Pty Ltd
14 15 16 17 18 19 20 19 18 17 16 15

Evaluated in independent research by staff from the
Department of Language, Literacy and Arts Education
at the University of Melbourne.

JOIN UP NOW!

Carmel Reilly

Contents

Chapter 1

JOINING A SPORTS TEAM

There are four good reasons for joining a sports team.

Being in a team:

- helps people to get better at their sport
- helps people to work together
- is a good way to keep fit and healthy
- is a good way to have fun with friends.

GETTING BETTER AT SPORT

Lots of people think that you have to be good at sport before you can join a team.
But this isn't true.
Sports teams play at many different levels,
so there are levels that are right for everyone.

When people join a team at the right level,
they get a lot of practice.

Getting a lot of practice helps people
to get better at sport.

Running Words 110

Chapter 3

WORKING TOGETHER

When people are part of a team,
they have to learn how to work together and get along.
Some players may be better than other players,
but everyone in a team has different **skills**.

The coach picks the right players
for the right places on the team.
This way, everyone gets to show their skills,
and improve as time goes on.

Chapter 4

BEING FIT AND HEALTHY

Playing a sport helps people to become fit and healthy.

People who are fit and healthy live longer and enjoy their lives.

Being fit also helps to make people feel better about who they are.

Many people think that they look and feel better
when they are fit.

Some people think that being fit
helps their minds work better, too!

FRIENDS

Being in a team
is a good way to spend time with people
who like the same things.

Being in a team is a good way to make friends.

Sometimes, people who are friends join a team together.
Sometimes, people make new friends in the team as time goes on.

Everyone can get a lot out of being in a team. Being part of a team is a good way to learn skills, get fit, and feel good all at the same time.

One of the most important things about being in a team
is to have fun!

Having fun is an important reason to join a team.
It's also a good reason to stay with a team for a long time.

Glossary

skills   talents that people have

Index